MANU, THE BOY WHO LOVED BIRDS

A Latitude 20 Book
University of Hawai'i Press
Honolulu

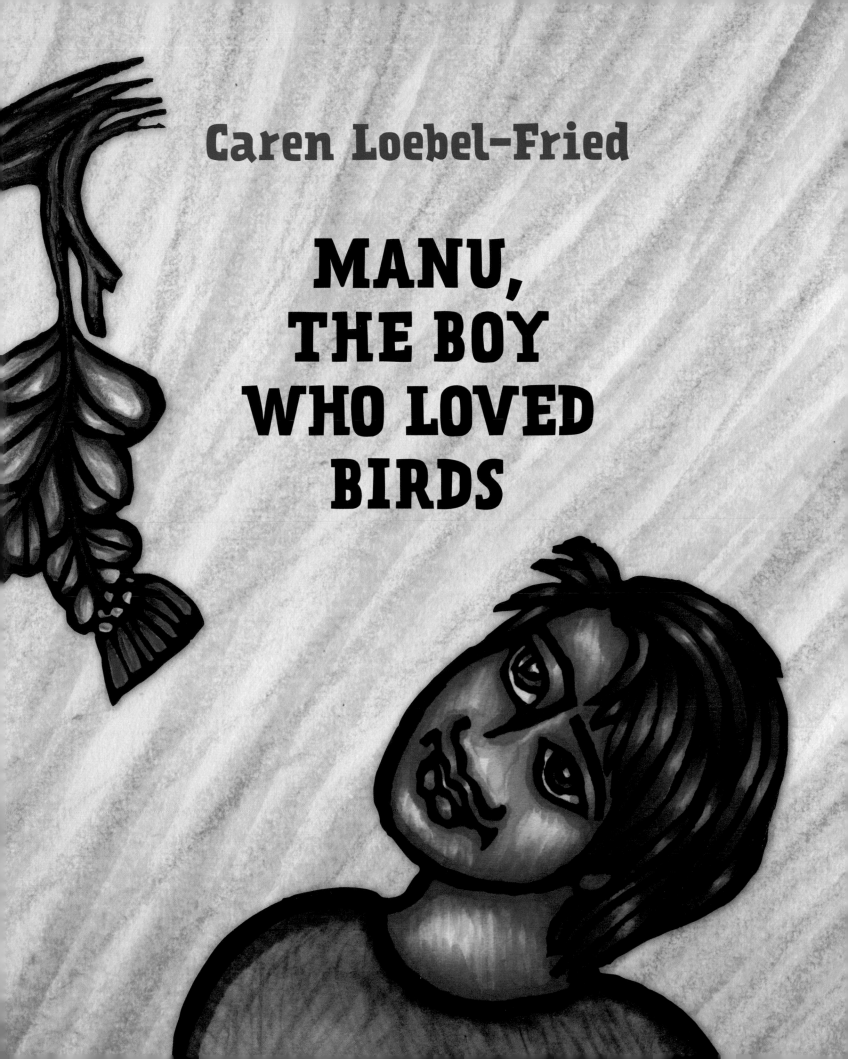

Caren Loebel-Fried

MANU, THE BOY WHO LOVED BIRDS

25 24 23 22 21 20   6 5 4 3 2 1

Library of Congress Cataloging-in-Publication Data

Names: Loebel-Fried, Caren, author, illustrator.

Title: Manu, the boy who loved birds / Caren Loebel-Fried.

Description: Honolulu : University of Hawai'i Press, [2020] | "A Latitude 20
book." | Summary: As he discovers the meaning of his Hawaiian name,
a young boy learns about an ancient, now extinct, Hawaiian forest bird
and the importance of bird conservation.

Identifiers: LCCN 2019033186 | ISBN 9780824882723 (hardback)

Subjects: CYAC: Birds—Fiction. | Honeyeaters—Fiction. | Extinct animals—
Fiction. | Wildlife conservation—Fiction. | Hawaii—Fiction.

Classification: LCC PZ7.L82545 Man 2020 | DDC [Fic]—dc23

LC record available at https://lccn.loc.gov/2019033186

University of Hawai'i Press books are printed on acid-free paper and meet the
guidelines for permanence and durability of the Council on Library Resources.

Design by Mardee Melton

Dedicated to all the children of the world,
who deserve forests full of diverse birds!

Manu squinted up at the sunny sky. A breeze tickled his cheek. He heard noisy clapping wings and watched a dove as she landed on a telephone wire. Puffing out her pretty spotted neck and tawny chest, she sang, "Hoo hi hooooo . . . Hoo!" Manu laughed. He loved birds!

Manu means *bird* in Hawaiian. A long time ago, Manu's father told him that his *full* name, Manuʻōʻōmauloa (Mah-noo-oh-oh-mow-low-uh) means, "May the ʻōʻō bird live on." His dad also said that ʻōʻō birds were extinct, gone forever.

That didn't make any sense.

Manu asked, "Why did you name me after a bird that is extinct? And if it's extinct, how can it still live on?"

His dad said, "Manu, names can have many meanings. Someday you will know what *your* name means to *you*."

Manu's class was learning about native Hawaiian forest birds. On a school trip to the Bishop Museum, he inspected the splendid feathered capes and headdresses, woven in bold yellow, red, and black stripes and zigzags.

Manu imagined himself as a powerful aliʻi, a high chief standing tall and strong in his feathered cloak and helmet, his ʻahu ʻula and mahiole. His people looked up at him with respect, waiting for a signal. Manu frowned. He looked out over the gray lava field, enemies in the distance fast approaching. He lifted his chin, ready for battle!

Suddenly, his friend Kimo interrupted Manu's imaginings. "Eh, Manuʻōʻō! Come see this skirt! It's made with a million ʻōʻō feathers. No wonder you don't have any yellow feathers left!" Everyone laughed.

Manu looked at the long feathered skirt. It was amazing! He was proud of his culture. But for the first time, he wondered: Where did all the ʻōʻō birds go?

That night, Manu told his father he wanted to know more about ʻōʻō birds. Together, they searched the internet and discovered many extraordinary things:

ʻŌʻō birds were endemic "honeyeaters" found in Hawaiʻi and nowhere else in the world.

ʻŌʻō birds flew in big flocks, from the sea up to the mountaintops, going where the flowers bloomed. They had tongues shaped like straws with a brush at the end for sucking nectar from the flowers. And they pollinated the flowers as they ate the nectar.

ʻŌʻō birds were tough and feisty, and often chased smaller birds away from nectar-filled flowers.

ʻŌʻō birds used to live close to where Manu's family lived now! There was once a native forest where now there were only buildings and roads . . . and lots of people.

Manu looked carefully at old paintings of ʻōʻō birds from the different Hawaiian Islands. There were four kinds of ʻōʻō.

Most had soft, glossy black plumage. The Hawaiʻi ʻōʻō, and Bishop's ʻōʻō from Mauiʻi and Molokaʻi, had fluffy yellow feathers peeking out from under each wing. The ʻōʻō from Kauaʻi had yellow feathers at the tops of their legs, like a little pair of shorts! But the Oʻahu ʻōʻō, the birds from *his* island, had yellow feathers along the sides of their bodies, and black and white striped tail feathers. Manu thought *his* ʻōʻō birds were the most beautiful of them all!

Manu and his dad found a library of bird songs from all over the world. In between the chirps of crickets and the whistles and tweets of other birds, Manu heard a strange song. It sounded like flutes echoed from outer space.

Manu suddenly realized, *this* was the song of the ʻōʻō!

Four Kinds of ʻŌʻō

Hawaiʻi   Oʻahu

Kauaʻi

Bishop's
(Maui and Molokaʻi)

That night, Manu had a dream about an ʻōʻō bird.

    With black feathers gleaming in the dim forest, ʻŌʻō sang in a loud clear voice. Then he cocked his head, listening. He heard his song repeated in the distance! ʻŌʻō answered, and then the two birds sang a duet, back and forth.

    ʻŌʻō flew closer to the song. He hopped quickly from branch to branch and dashed to the end of a reaching limb. Crouching low, he cocked his head to listen. Suddenly, he couldn't move his feet. He was stuck to the branch! ʻŌʻō tried desperately to escape. A human hand appeared and pulled ʻŌʻō from the branch, holding him firmly. ʻŌʻō was terrified. Fingers plucked yellow feathers from the sides of his body, then wiped the glue from his feet. The hand opened and ʻŌʻō flew wildly up and up as fast as he could, tearing through tangled leaves and branches—

    Manu woke suddenly. His heart was racing.

    His dream seemed so real! Manu thought about the ʻōʻō bird. He wished the feathers of all the beautiful forest birds had been drab and plain.

The next day, Manu's teacher told his class to try and imagine what the history of Hawai'i might have been like from an 'ō'ō bird's perspective.

"Millions of years ago, a black bird from a faraway land was migrating with a group of her relatives. They got caught in a terrible storm and strong winds carried them out to sea, far from their usual route. After days and miles of flying through gusts and raging wind, the air finally calmed. They saw a dark shape on the horizon and flew to a strange land of lava. She and her flock hungrily ate nectar and flowers from a few small trees. They plucked tiny insects from the leaves, branches, and under the bark. Exhausted, they settled in the tree for the night. She slept for the first time in her new homeland.

"Others had already discovered this remote island chain. Seabirds nested and raised their young here in safety, far from animals that could harm them. Shorebirds and waterfowl had also arrived. Seeds came with birds, some stuck on their feathers and feet, and some from fruit in their bellies. Insects also traveled here by wind and ocean currents, and some floated across the ocean on debris.

"One by one, over thousands of years, birds, insects, seeds, snails, and bats arrived here. Birds pollinated the plants as they ate the nectar and flowers and helped spread seeds when they ate the fruit. Over time, huge forests grew across the land. The 'ō'ō and all the other pioneers became ancestors to the endemic species of Hawai'i. They adapted and changed over time, and depended on each other for survival.

"And then, about 1,000 years ago, humans from Polynesia voyaged by canoe and settled here. Over time, they were joined by people from other parts of the world. Humans brought plants and animals that were useful to their ways of life, like chickens, cows, sheep, goats, pigs, cats, and dogs. They also carried stowaways to these islands, like rats, mice, and mosquitoes. Forests were cleared for crops. Endemic plants were crowded out by newly introduced plants, and native saplings were trampled and eaten. Introduced animals ate Hawai'i's native birds, their eggs, and their young. And birds were bitten by mosquitoes and infected with deadly diseases.

"And now, many of our endemic Hawaiian plants and animals are gone."

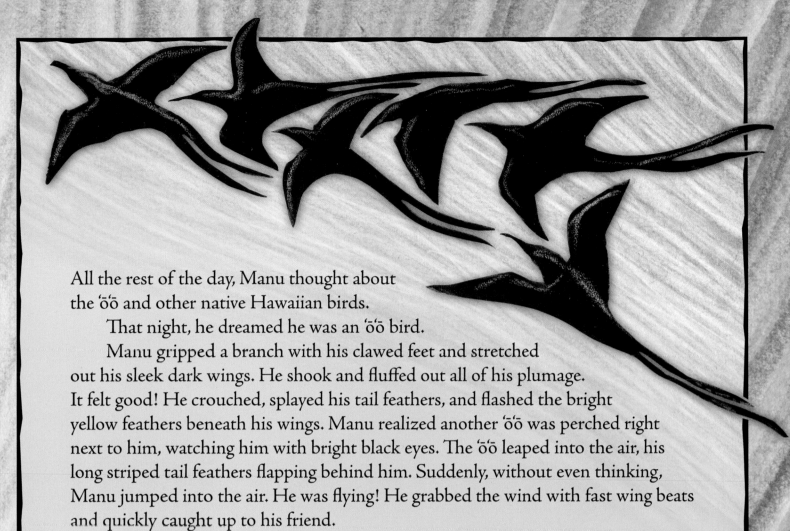

All the rest of the day, Manu thought about
the ʻōʻō and other native Hawaiian birds.

That night, he dreamed he was an ʻōʻō bird.

Manu gripped a branch with his clawed feet and stretched
out his sleek dark wings. He shook and fluffed out all of his plumage.
It felt good! He crouched, splayed his tail feathers, and flashed the bright
yellow feathers beneath his wings. Manu realized another ʻōʻō was perched right
next to him, watching him with bright black eyes. The ʻōʻō leaped into the air, his
long striped tail feathers flapping behind him. Suddenly, without even thinking,
Manu jumped into the air. He was flying! He grabbed the wind with fast wing beats
and quickly caught up to his friend.

They banked around lush fern trees, spiraling playfully over the mossy forest
floor. Manu felt like he was the pilot *and* the plane, doing crazy tricks! They zipped
through the sweet, damp air, taking turns chasing each other. ʻŌlapa trees, like
hula dancers, waved their leaves gracefully as Manu and the ʻōʻō bird flew by. Manu
quickly plucked and swallowed an ʻōlapa berry, then caught up to his friend to help
chase smaller birds away from lehua blossoms. They slurped up the sweet nectar.
Manu thought it tasted like liquid candy.

The two birds flew up to the open sky, sailing in graceful arcs over the treetops.
As they traveled the forest started to grow thin. Manu felt hungry. They searched
for flowers, but there were few.

They flew and flew, up the mountain. Suddenly, Manu noticed he was flying
alone. Where did his friend go? Manu looked everywhere! He frantically searched
the sky, then the treetops below, screaming, **"OH-OH!
OH-OH!"**

"Manu 'ō'ō!"

Manu opened his eyes. His mother held him. He scanned his bedroom, searching wildly for the 'ō'ō bird. "Manu, it's ok! You were dreaming!"

Manu blinked.

He was quiet, remembering.

Then he said, "I dreamed that all the forests were gone and there was no food for the forest birds! Mom, are there still forests in Hawai'i for the native birds? Will I ever get to see a Hawaiian forest bird?"

Manu's mother touched his cheek gently. "Yes, Manu. Your dad and I have a surprise for your birthday. We are going to the Island of Hawai'i to visit our Big Island 'ohana. There, we will go to the native forest and see the birds!"

Manu hugged his mother tightly. He thought secretly, "And there I will find the 'ō'ō bird. Then I'll learn the meaning of my name!"

The day finally came.

Uncle picked up Manu and his parents at the Hilo airport. The family arrived to a lūʻau. Cousins and friends sang and played ʻukulele and guitars. Tūtū danced a hula called "Manu ʻŌʻō" in honor of Manu's birthday. Manu ate his favorite foods: pork laulau and haupia for dessert. But all through the party, Manu kept thinking about the next day when he would finally see the native birds.

In the morning, Manu and his family went to Hawai'i Volcanoes National Park. At the visitor center, they explored displays of the park's forest plants and birds. Manu pressed buttons to hear the songs and calls of these birds. He listened over and over again, memorizing their sounds.

Out on the trail, the air felt cool and misty. The forest smelled sweet. Through the leaves, they could see Kīlauea Volcano puffing steamy clouds into the sky. Manu was excited and looked at everything around him. But he had learned from his parents to be quiet and still, to look and listen.

Manu heard whirring wings and whispered, "'Apapane!" Their bubbly song filled the forest. He could see them through his dad's binoculars, their red bodies and white vent feathers easy to identify. Manu watched one 'apapane land right above them and plunge his beak into a bright red lehua blossom.

Manu whispered, "'Ōma'o!" He recognized their song, which sounded just like their name. But Manu couldn't find the 'ōma'o bird through the binoculars. His father said quietly, "The 'ōma'o are very shy, and their gray feathers make them blend into the shadows. But we know they are near when we hear their song."

Then they saw an 'io, a Hawaiian hawk, gliding in big circles high up in the sky. Its calls pierced the air. **"Zzeee-ir! Zzeee-ir!"**

That afternoon, Manu and his parents visited a special conservation center where endangered Hawaiian forest birds were being raised. Someday, these rare birds would be released back into the wild. Manu learned about the plants and insects these birds depended on for food. To survive in the wild, they would have to find food on their own.

Manu saw big Hawaiian crows, ʻalalā, in a room with screened windows that was filled with trees. They hopped heavily from branch to branch. One made funny muttering sounds and watched another who pecked at a hole in a tree trunk. Manu walked down a dark hallway, where windows revealed rooms that looked like little forests. These environments had been created for the endangered birds so they could grow in safety. Manu watched the ʻakikiki, then the kiwikiu. He paused and smiled at the palila with their bright yellow heads, zipping from branches to food bowls, so funny and cute. One palila seemed to look right at Manu! Squinting his eyes, Manu imagined the walls disappearing and the palila flying free.

Manu felt so happy to be surrounded by Hawaiian birds and plants. But then he realized he had not seen any ʻōʻō birds that whole day! Were the ʻōʻō really gone?

It was their last morning on Hawai'i Island. Manu's family drove up the slope of Mauna Kea. The mountain wore a little white cap of snow on top!

They were going as volunteers to plant koa trees inside a large area that was surrounded by a tall fence. Their project leader explained, "When we protect an area from predators, remove invasive weeds and restore the native and endemic plants, the Hawaiian plants will grow and thrive. Then, the native birds and insects will come! The birds always tell us about our forests. When lots of different birds are living in a forest, we know that forest is healthy."

The earth felt cool and damp in Manu's hands. In the distance, he saw a giant old koa tree. Manu looked down at the reaching roots of the tiny sapling he held gently between his fingers. Manu spoke quietly. "Hey, keiki. Little koa baby! Someday you'll grow big, too!"

That night, in his own bed, Manu drifted off to sleep.

He dreamed he was in a very old forest. The koa and ʻōhiʻa trees grew so close together, Manu could barely see the sky. The air felt fresh and cool. Manu heard a familiar song and looked up. There was ʻŌʻō, perched on a branch, watching Manu! ʻŌʻō cocked his head and flicked his tail feathers. Manu smiled at his friend.

Suddenly, a big flock of ʻōʻō birds flew overhead calling, "Oh! Oh!" Manu was amazed to see so many ʻōʻō birds. The birds flew low, and their wings made a buzzing sound. His friend looked up at the other ʻōʻō birds, and then at Manu again. Then, ʻŌʻō leaped off the branch and flew up to join his flock. Manu watched as all the ʻōʻō birds flew together. They called, "Oh! Oh!" as they made smooth waves over the tops of the trees. Their black feathers glistened in the sunshine as they flew into the distance. And then they were gone.

Manu opened his eyes. Bright sunshine filled his bedroom with light. Manu thought about his dream. He said quietly, "'Ō'ō, I will never forget you."

At breakfast, Manu told his father and mother about his dream. He said, "I realize now, the 'ō'ō birds are really gone." He sighed, "It makes me so sad."

But then, Manu brightened. "I also know there are other native birds still here, and they need our help! They need the forest to survive!"

Excited, Manu said, "I can plant native trees, and get my friends to help, too!" His parents smiled and nodded.

Then Manu was quiet.

He thought about his Hawaiian name and its English translation.

Manu'ō'ōmauloa: May the 'ō'ō bird live on.

Manu thought about 'Ō'ō, the bird in his dreams. He remembered dream-flying with 'Ō'ō through the forest. Manu closed his eyes and felt himself soaring through the air, the wind rushing through his black feathered wings . . .

Manu opened his eyes.

He started to smile.

He looked at his mom and dad.

"I just realized . . . even though the 'ō'ō birds are gone, they will always live on in *me* . . . in my dreams . . . and in my name!"

And that was when Manu finally understood the meaning of his name.

Male and Female Oahu O-o, *Moho apicalis.*
Illustration by John Gerrard Keulemans in
The Avifauna of Laysan and the Neighboring Islands,
by the Honorable Walter Rothschild, 1893.

Afterword

The Hawaiian Islands are a very small part of the United States, covering only 0.2 percent of the land. But, Hawai'i is home to 20 percent of the endangered or threatened birds in the United States. Many of Hawai'i's birds have gone extinct. A long time ago, there were four different species of 'ō'ō birds living on their own islands: O'ahu, Hawai'i, Maui and Moloka'i, and Kaua'i. In the 1980s, the Kaua'i 'ō'ō was the last of the 'ō'ō to be seen or heard.

The details about the 'ō'ō bird in this story are based on the research and observations of biologists, early explorers and collectors, artists, and Hawaiian cultural stories and proverbs. The descriptions of the birds are mostly about Manu's favorite, the O'ahu 'ō'ō, but include information about all four species of 'ō'ō birds.

The 'ō'ō are the oldest lineage of Hawaiian forest birds, dating back fourteen to seventeen million years. Most of the 'ō'ō birds were extinct before photography was invented. We know what the 'ō'ō looked like because of the artists who captured their beauty in paintings, and from museum collections of the birds.

Forest birds were considered sacred by the Hawaiian people. The 'ō'ō birds were listed in the Kumulipo, the Hawaiian Creation Chant, recognized in Hawaiian cultural history as part of the fabric and origin of all creatures on earth.

Singers in the Forest

The ʻōʻō were songbirds. They were considered to be the finest singers of all native Hawaiian birds. The male and female ʻōʻō were known to sing duets together. Their song was flutelike, and their call was a loud "OH! OH!" like their name. They sang mostly in the morning and evening, especially during breeding season.

Hear the song of the Kauaʻi ʻōʻō!
Visit https://macaulaylibrary.org/asset/6049.

(From the Macaulay Library at the Cornell Lab of Ornithology, recorded on June 6, 1975, copyright C. Fred Zeillemaker.)

What Did the ʻŌʻō Birds Eat?

ʻŌʻō were mostly nectar feeders of the forest canopy. They foraged from sea level all the way up to the mountaintops, following the blooming flowers. They also ate insects that they found on branches, trunks, twigs, and leaves of living and dead trees like koa, ʻōhiʻa, and ʻōlapa. Their favorite flowers were the lehua blossoms from the ʻōhiʻa tree, but they sucked nectar from other flowers like Lobelias, kanawao plants, ʻieʻie, and banana flowers. They also ate banana fruit. ʻŌʻō pollinated plants as they ate the nectar, so they helped the plants as the plants fed them.

Hawaiian Words and Names in This Story

'Ahu 'ula
(ah-hoo ooh-luh)

Hawaiian feather cape or cloak

'Apapane
(ah-pah-pah-nay)

Small, bright red Hawaiian forest bird

'Io
(ee-oh)

Hawaiian hawk

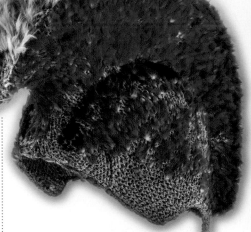

Ali'i
(ah-lee-ee)

Hawaiian high chief

Keiki
(kay-kee)

Child

Mahiole
(mah-hee-oh-lay)

Hawaiian feather helmet

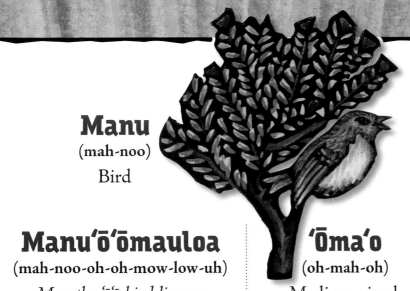

Manu
(mah-noo)

Bird

Po'e Kia Manu
(po-ay kee-yuh mah-noo)

Feather hunter

Manu'ō'ōmauloa
(mah-noo-oh-oh-mow-low-uh)

May the 'ō'ō bird live on

'Ōma'o
(oh-mah-oh)

Medium-sized,
gray forest bird

Tūtū
(too-too)

Grandparent or elder

Mauna Kea
(mow-nah kay-ah)

An ancient volcanic mountain
on the Island of Hawai'i
and the tallest peak in the
Hawaiian Islands; its name
can mean "white mountain"
or "snow mountain"

'Ō'ō
(oh-oh)

Hawaiian forest bird,
extinct; its name
means "to pierce"

'Ōlapa
(oh-lah-pah)

Native Hawaiian tree with
leaves that wave in the
breeze like a hula dancer's
hands; its name means
"hula dancer"

Bird Feathers in Old Hawai'i

Certain feathers, mostly from forest birds, were very valuable in ancient Hawai'i. Feathers were tied in little bundles and used to pay taxes. Forest birds and their feathers were honored by Hawaiian people and believed to represent and hold the spirits of the gods. Feathers were considered to be powerful and were used by high chiefs to aid them in battles. Feathers were also the symbol of royalty.

Hawaiian featherwork was a fine art in the old days. Capes, cloaks, and lei were made with bright red feathers from the 'i'iwi and 'apapane birds, green feathers from the 'ō'ū, and the black and yellow feathers of the mamo. But the most valuable feathers were the yellow underwing, thigh, and flank feathers of the 'ō'ō, saved for the high chiefs and kings.

Poʻe Kia Manu is the Hawaiian name for feather hunters who worked for the aliʻi collecting feathers from the birds. They had an important job and did it well. The hunters learned the bird's behavior so they could track and trap them. Feather hunters would smear a stick or branch with a sticky glue-like substance from the seed pods of the pāpala kēpau, the Pisonia tree, and mimic the birds to attract them. The ʻōʻō would respond to the imitations of their calls. Birds were also caught with nets and snares. The hunters were careful not to hurt the birds. Most of the time, they could pluck the feathers needed and then set the birds free. Sometimes the ʻōʻō birds would be eaten after the feathers were taken. But most often, especially once the birds became rare, they were set free with the hope that they would survive and grow new valuable feathers.

The yellow skirt that Manu saw at the Bishop Museum is called the Pāʻū of Nāhiʻenaʻena. When it was first made, this skirt measured twenty feet long by thirty inches wide. It is thought to be the largest piece of Hawaiian featherwork ever created, made with almost one million yellow feathers from the ʻōʻō bird.

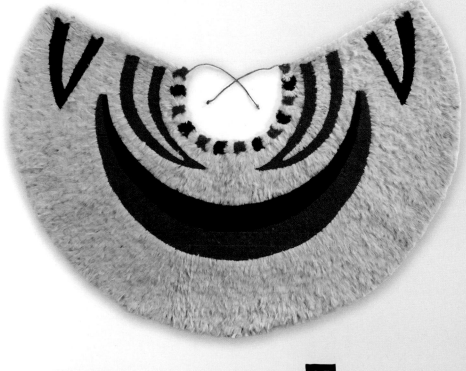

How Can We Help?

Extinction is forever.

There are things we can do to help native species! Here are some ways we can make a difference:

* Learn about native species.

* Go on a bird-watching hike.

* Clean your boots, socks, and other clothing after hiking to prevent the spread of weeds and the fungus that causes Rapid ʻŌhiʻa Death.

* Join a wildlife organization and get involved by donating, participating in activities, and volunteering. Kauaʻi Forest Bird Recovery Project, Maui Forest Bird Recovery Project, Pacific Rim Conservation, Hawaiʻi Wildlife Center, and the ʻAlalā Project all work to help restore Hawaiʻi's endangered birds.

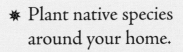

* Volunteer with an organization that does habitat restoration. On Hawaiʻi Island, Mauna Kea Forest Restoration Project is an organization that brings volunteers on outplanting field trips, and Hakalau Forest National Wildlife Refuge has volunteer planting opportunities.

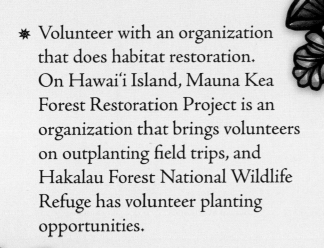

* Plant native species around your home.

* Keep your pets indoors or fenced in your yard. Dogs and cats kill birds.

* Never release unwanted cats, dogs, birds, or other animals into the wild.

* Stop the spread of mosquitoes and avian diseases. Around your house, remove or cover things that collect rainwater where mosquitoes can breed, like flower pots, clogged gutters, and old tires.

* Help to slow climate change by walking or taking the bus instead of driving. Turn off your house lights, television, and computer when not in use.

* Intern, volunteer, or join the team as a staff member at Keauhou Bird Conservation Center, in Volcano, Hawaiʻi.

Acknowledgments

Mahalo to Rick, Alex, and Kaʻōʻōmauloa, whose real story is the inspiration for this book.

Deepest thanks to the late Marjorie Ziegler, who conceived of the idea for this story, partnered on early versions, supported its development, and never let it go extinct.

Warmest appreciation to Thane Pratt, who enthusiastically reviewed the ʻōʻō art and generously shared information that helped bring the ʻōʻō to life, including field notes from a 1976 survey of "ʻŌʻō Valley" in the ʻAlakaʻi Swamp, Kauaʻi. Many thanks to Paul Banko, who roused the living ʻōʻō with stories from him and his father and their close observations of ʻōʻō behavior. Thank you to Julie Williams and Jack Jeffrey, who shared their ʻōʻō experiences with me. Thank you to Megan Dalton and Mary Berman, who reviewed the story for scientific and cultural accuracy. Big thanks to Chris Farmer and Stephanie Levins, who helped awaken the art in the dream sequences. And sincere thanks to two anonymous readers for their helpful comments and critiques.

Heartfelt thanks to Joel Cosseboom at University of Hawaiʻi Press for his creative vision and passion for this story. Much appreciation to Bryce Masuda at Keauhou Bird Conservation Center for sharing his work with Hawaiʻi's endangered forest birds and their recovery. And thank you to the Bishop Museum for carefully preserving cultural artifacts and the skins of extinct forest birds, so we can always know the treasures that have been lost and take care of those that still remain.

This book was made possible with help from Conservation Council for Hawaiʻi. The Conservation Council for Hawaiʻi is dedicated to protecting native Hawaiian plants, animals, and ecosystems for future generations. Ko Hawaiʻi leo no nā holoholona lōhiu—Hawaiʻi's voice for wildlife.

conservationcouncilhawaii.org

Illustration Credits

All illustrations are by the author, except as noted below.

Page 32

TOP LEFT: 'Ahu 'ula (feathered cloak of nobility) made from red 'i'iwi feathers and yellow and black feathers from the 'ō'ō. Photo by Hal Lum and Masayo Suzuki, Bishop Museum Archives.

BOTTOM LEFT: High Chief Boki and his wife, High Chiefess Liliha. Painting by J. Hayter, ca. 1824, Bishop Museum Archives.

TOP RIGHT: Three 'apapane perched on branches of the yellow 'ōhi'a lehua tree. Hand-colored lithograph by William Frohawk published in *Aves Hawaiienses: The Birds of the Sandwich Islands*, by S. B. Wilson and A. H. Evans, 1891, Bishop Museum Archives.

BOTTOM RIGHT: Mahiole (feathered helmet) made from red feathers from the 'i'iwi bird and yellow feathers from the 'ō'ō bird. Photo by Hal Lum and Masayo Suzuki, Bishop Museum Archives.

Page 33

BOTTOM RIGHT: Painting of an 'ō'ō bird. Watercolor by Sarah Stone, ca. 1783, Bishop Museum Archives.

Page 34

Lei hulu (feathered lei) made from the black and yellow feathers from the 'ō'ō and red feathers of the 'i'iwi. Photo by Hal Lum and Masayo Suzuki, Bishop Museum Archives.

Page 35

LEFT: 'Ahu 'ula (feathered cape) made from yellow and black feathers of the 'ō'ō and red feathers of the 'i'iwi. Photo by Hal Lum and Masayo Suzuki, Bishop Museum Archives.

RIGHT: Painting of composite feather lei made with yellow, red, black, and white feathers. Watercolor by Sarah Stone, ca. 1783, Bishop Museum Archives.

About the Author

Caren Keʻalaokapualehua Loebel-Fried is an award-winning author and artist from Volcano, Hawaiʻi. Birds, conservation, culture, and the natural world are foundations for her work. Caren has created seven storybooks to date, including *Hawaiian Legends of the Guardian Spirits*, *A Perfect Day for an Albatross*, and *Lono and the Magical Land Beneath the Sea*, which incorporate the ancient art of block printing, taught to her by her mother. Caren's books have been recipients of the American Folklore Society's Aesop Prize for Children's Folklore and the Ka Palapala Poʻokela Award. Caren exhibits art and gives presentations about her work throughout Hawaiʻi and the continental United States. Her commissions for iconic and educational art include the United States Fish & Wildlife Service, Midway Atoll National Wildlife Refuge, Kīlauea Point Natural History Association, Conservation Council for Hawaiʻi, and private collectors. Caren spent five weeks on Midway Atoll counting and researching albatrosses. Through art and story, Caren aims to bring people, especially children, closer to the natural world with the hope that they will want to help care for it.